Twiggy,
Story of a Greyhound

By Ginny Anne Folkman

Illustrations by Chrysa Neas

EMERALD
P R E S S

Dedicated in loving memory of my son Corby.
And to my little niece Amber.

Special Thanks to
David Wolf of National Greyhound Adoption,
Candy Durante, Janet Hall, Mary Sherkness, Air Flair Fritz,
Kim Dugan, Ann Durante (Twiggy's babysitter),
my sister Barbara, my mother, and most of all my husband George.

·PREFACE

Greyhounds are the fastest of dogs and one of the oldest of breeds. A streamline, slender but strong dog, the greyhound can attain a speed of over 40 miles per hour. They are also very loving affectionate animals, and they are very good with children.

Greyhound racing is a so-called 20th century sport. The greyhound chases by sight and is called a sighthound. They are raced around an enclosed track in pursuit of an electrically-controlled and propelled mechanical rabbit. People wager money on the outcome of the race. Oliver P. Smith demonstrated the sport in 1919 at Emeryville, California, and the first track opened at St. Petersburg, Florida in 1925. The sport was introduced in England in 1926 and became more popular there than in the United States. In the United States dog races were at first held only in Florida and Massachusetts, but by the 1980's the sport had spread to many other states. There are 56 Greyhound Tracks in 18 states. Greyhound racing raises money for the State Treasuries where they race.

Greyhounds are raced only for as long as they win races. When they don't win any more, they are destroyed — tens of thousands each year. But, thanks to people who care, there are many greyhounds saved from this fate. This is a story of one greyhound who found a happy home and beat the odds.

Chapter 1 – *THE RACE*

It was the last race of the night and it would be the last race for Twiggy if she didn't win any money this time. It had been awhile since Twiggy was in the winner's circle. Tonight the number she was wearing was Number Three. As her trainer walked her to the starting gate, Twiggy thought to herself, "I have to win tonight or they'll send me to that place from where you never come back."

The race was about to start. "And they're off!" the announcer cried. As she was running, Twiggy could feel her heart pumping fast and her muscles burning more than they had ever burned before. She felt she had never run faster. She was sure she would win tonight.

As they were coming around the first bend, Twiggy thought "I'm going to catch that rabbit tonight." But, Twiggy was back in fourth place and it seemed impossible for her to go any faster even though she was trying her hardest. "And they're in the final stretch, and Number Seven is in the lead, Number Five is in second place, Number Ten is in third place and Number Three is in fourth place," Twiggy heard over the loudspeaker. "And they're coming to the finish line, and it's Number Seven, Number Seven is the winner!"

Twiggy couldn't believe it. She thought she could win, she was so close. She had put everything she had into that race.

As her trainer walked her back to the kennel, Twiggy had a tear in her eye. She didn't sleep very well that night. All she could think of was that terrible place.

Chapter 2 – *SAYING GOOD-BYE*

The next morning, Twiggy could hardly move. Her muscles were so sore. She heard the door open. I have some good news," her trainer said. "You are going up North to live! Somewhere in Pennsylvania. It's not as warm as you are used to, and it snows in the winter and gets real cold, but you'll adjust."

"Snow," Twiggy wondered. "What's snow? What's Pennsylvania? What's cold?"

"At least you're not going to the pound," her trainer assured her. "You will be leaving tomorrow for your new home, thanks to the 'National Greyhound Adoption Program.' Come on Twiggy, let's take a walk." Twiggy walked close to her trainer. She really liked him. She was going to miss him, but she wasn't sure if he would miss her. He had trained so many like her. So many had gone before her.

That night after dinner, all her friends got together and had a going-away party for Twiggy. All her closest friends were there — Woody, Breezy, Co Co. "We're all going to miss you, Twiggy," Woody said sadly. "But at least you're not going to that place they sent Paisley and Maggie!"

"I know," Twiggy said. "I am grateful to have a home to go to, but I really am going to miss all of you. You are the only friends I ever had. How will I ever make new friends in a strange place! I don't think I'll ever find friends as good as you."

Chapter 3 — *THE PLANE RIDE*

The next morning Twiggy's trainer got her ready for the trip up north. What Twiggy didn't know was that she was going by airplane which would be a new experience for her. As they were putting Twiggy on board the plane, she was concerned what might be ahead for her. It would seem like the longest journey of her life. But the ride was more comfortable than the old trucks she rode in. She had a lot of time to think. As she lay in her travel cage, she thought of her life in Florida as a racer.

She remembered the first time her trainer put a rabbit in front of her. Instinctively, she knew to chase it. She was very fast in her early years. She would work so hard to win each race she was in. She did win many races, but it seemed the rise to stardom didn't last very long. Twiggy had no idea of what continuing to lose would mean until one day they took her sister and six other dogs away in an old truck she didn't recognize. Her sister Maggie never returned. Twiggy was one of the fortunate ones. She had a home to go to and a whole new life ahead of her. But Twiggy would never forget the ones she left behind at the racetrack.

When they took Twiggy off the plane she had a worried look on her face. It was so cold outside. It was the beginning of December. She was so cold her teeth were chattering.

She had heard her trainer say as they were putting her on the plane that her new family would be waiting for her at the airport. "I hope they like me" Twiggy wished.

Chapter 4 — *TWIGGY'S NEW FAMILY*

Her new family was like any other average family. There was George, who was the father; Ginger, who was the mother, and two children – Mikie, twelve years old and Linda, who was ten years old.

As Twiggy was walked through the airport, she was more and more excited about meeting her new family. Then she heard someone shout, "That must be her!" It was George, Twiggy's new father.

"She's so skinny!" Mikie said poutingly. "I wanted a real dog, a black lab. That dog is ugly."

"You be nice. She needs a home," Ginger sternly said.

"I think she's cute," Linda said with a big smile on her face.

Twiggy had heard what Mikie said. "Oh, no – he hates me. What do I do now?" Twiggy thought. She did the only thing she could do to let him know she wanted him to like her. She walked over to where Mikie was sitting and put her head on his lap and looked up at him with her big, brown, sad eyes, and then she licked his face. She did melt his heart a little bit, but she knew it would take some time to win his heart completely. After all, she had to compete with a big strong Lab.

"What's her name?" Linda asked.

"They told us her name was Twiggy," Ginger answered.

"Twiggy! Oh brother!" Mikie said with disgust in his voice.

"I think it's a perfect name for her. She looks like she's as skinny as the twigs on my favorite tree in our backyard, and that's what I'm going to call her," Linda replied.

"Yes, we'll keep her name. She's used to that name," Ginger said.

"At least I'll have something I'm used to being called," Twiggy thought.

"Come on, let's get Twiggy home where it's warm. She's shaking," George said with concern in his voice.

"Can I sit with Twiggy on the way home? I'll keep her warm," Linda begged.

"All right, Linda, but don't crowd her or make her nervous," Ginger replied.

"I'll go get the car, you all wait here," George said.

Chapter 5 — *THE RIDE HOME*

All the way home Twiggy looked out the window to see what Pennsylvania was like. It wasn't like Florida. There weren't any palm trees and the land wasn't as flat. There were so many rolling hills and there were trees that looked as if they were covered with green needles.

There were many small towns in Pennsylvania. Sumneytown was where her new family lived.

"You're going to like Sumneytown, Twiggy. You'll have a nice big backyard to play in and lots of woods around the house to explore," George assured her.

"What's a backyard? What are woods?" Twiggy

wondered. All she knew was her kennel and the sand racetrack.

The car pulled down a long, winding, stone driveway up to a big, white, two-story house with a wraparound porch. Twiggy remembered seeing houses before when her trainer would take her for walks, but they were all one-story. She had never seen a house like this before. It almost looked like a house you would see in a storybook.

"Here we are. Your new home, Twiggy," George said.

As Twiggy looked around, she didn't see a kennel or a cage.

"I wonder where I'll sleep tonight?" Twiggy thought.

As Twiggy got out of the car and stepped onto the driveway, the stones felt funny under her paws. It wasn't like the sand track she raced on, or the cement floor of her kennel. She gently walked across the driveway onto the brick path that led to the big white house.

"Come on, Twiggy. Come see your new home," Linda said as she pulled Twiggy toward the front door. As Twiggy walked up the front steps onto the porch, she did so very carefully. She had never walked up steps before. Linda laughed at her clumsiness.

"Bring her inside," Ginger shouted from in the house. Mikie was still in the driveway watching Twiggy and how clumsily she was walking up the steps.

"What a dumb dog!" he said quietly to himself. "What are my friends going to think of her? They all have German Shepherds and Labs. I'll be the joke of the neighborhood when they see her."

Meanwhile, Twiggy was sniffing from room to room. The carpet felt so soft under her paws. "Linda, show Twiggy where her water bowl is and come help me feed her. She must be hungry after her long trip," Ginger called from the kitchen. Twiggy walked over to the bowl of food that Linda put down for her. She sniffed what was inside, but she was so excited she couldn't even eat.

"Mom, can Twiggy sleep in my room?" Linda pleaded.

"Okay. Put the bed we bought for her in your room," Ginger replied.

"What's a bed?" Twiggy wondered. "I'm used to sleeping on a cement floor."

Linda brought Twiggy's bed into her room. It was like a big bean bag and it smelled like cedar. Linda put an old quilt on top of the canvas bed so it would be nice and soft for her.

"Come over and try your new bed, Twiggy," Linda said as she patted her hand on the bed. Twiggy walked over, stepped on the bed and turned around in circles until she found just the right spot, and flopped down with a grunt!

"This feels so good!" Twiggy thought. She was tired from her long journey. Linda patted her on the head and said, "You sleep now Twiggy. You'll have a big day tomorrow." Twiggy's eyes closed very slowly. She never felt so warm and snug.

Chapter 6 — *TWIGGY'S FIRST DAY*

When Twiggy opened her eyes, it was the next morning. She had slept all through the night.

"What is that wonderful smell?" she wondered. It smelled so delicious. Linda was still sleeping so Twiggy got up and quietly walked toward the aroma. As she entered the kitchen, Ginger greeted her saying, "Good morning sleepy head. I have a special treat for your first morning here." Ginger put Twiggy's bowl down and inside was bacon and eggs. Twiggy lapped it right up. She didn't remember anything tasting so good. As Mikie was eating his breakfast, Ginger said, "Why don't you take Twiggy to meet some of your friends after school?"

"Mom, do I have to?" Mikie whined.

"Oh come on Mikie. Maybe you could show them how fast she runs. I'll drop Linda and Twiggy off at football practice after school." Ginger tried to be convincing.

"But Mom, the kids are going to laugh at me for having a dog that looks like her."

"Well, they're going to see her sooner or later. It may as well be today." Ginger said.

Mikie grabbed his books and left in a huff. After school, Ginger dropped Linda and Twiggy off at football practice. Mikie was already there with his friends — Jesse, Ryan and Kenny, and Linda's friend, Becky, was waiting for her. Kenny was there with his big German shepherd, Max. As Twiggy got out of the car, Kenny said, "What is that?"

"It's an ugly dog, it's so skinny!" Kenny added.

"Oh yeah! I bet she can outrun your dog by a mile." Mikie snapped back at Kenny.

"You really think so?" Kenny asked with a snicker. "Well, let's see who has the fastest dog then." Kenny said, thinking it would be no contest. "Let's have a race."

"Okay, you're on!" Mikie said. Mikie never saw Twiggy run, but after all, she had been a race dog. "Linda, you and Becky go to the other end of the field with Jesse and Ryan. Kenny and I will stay at this end and let the dogs go." Mikie yelled.

Twiggy looked at the huge dog next to her and thought, "I never raced with a dog like this before. I never even saw a dog like this before. I hope he can't run faster than I can. He sure is a lot bigger than me. If it will get Mikie to like me, I'll do my best to beat this dog."

"Okay, let them go," Ryan yelled across the field. Mikie and Kenny let the dogs go and Twiggy took off like a bullet.

"Come on Twiggy," Linda was yelling. "You can do it. You can beat him." Linda kept yelling. As they ran toward Linda and Becky, Max was falling farther and farther behind Twiggy. It was no contest just as Kenny had thought, but it was Twiggy who beat Max by twenty yards. Ryan, Jesse, Linda and Becky were cheering. Even Mikie had a proud look on his face.

"Your dog is really neat," Ryan said. Everyone agreed. "What kind of dog is it?" they asked.

"She's a greyhound," Linda replied as she was hugging Twiggy's neck.

"She's really a neat looking dog with those brown and black stripes. She looks like a tiger," Becky said admiringly.

"I bet she could run faster than a tiger," Linda proudly said.

As Kenny and Mikie walked over to where the others were, Kenny said, as he was looking down, "Well, your dog won the race fair and square. I never saw a dog run so fast. Where did you get her?"

"My Mom and Dad saw an ad in the paper for ex-race dogs who needed a home. Twiggy used to race at the Greyhound Races in Florida. The people we got her from said they only race them as long as they continue winning and when they don't win races anymore, they send them to the pound to be destroyed. There's a special group called the 'National Greyhound Adoption Program' that finds homes for them all over the United States," Mikie answered as Kenny listened with real interest.

"That was a really nice thing for your parents to do. She can really run fast, but she still looks funny," Kenny said jokingly.

"Well, you know the old saying — you can't judge a book by its cover," Mikie said. Even though Mikie heard those words come out of his own mouth, he wasn't sure he felt that way about Twiggy in his heart.

"Are you going to play hockey this Saturday? We're going to play on the pond behind my house," Mikie informed Kenny.

"Sure. I'll be there. Can I bring Max? Are you bringing Twiggy?" Kenny asked.

Mikie thought to himself for a minute. "My Mom said if Twiggy is outside for a long time, she has to wear a coat because her hair is short and she's so skinny. The kids will laugh at her and at me for having a dog so goofy looking." After a long pause he answered, "I don't know if I'm bringing Twiggy, but you can bring Max if you want."

"Come on Mikie, Dad's here," Linda yelled.

As they all got into the car, Linda was so excited when she told her Dad how Twiggy beat Max in the race.

"Dad, you should have seen Twiggy. She ran so fast, she beat Max by a mile." As Twiggy heard Linda tell the story, she felt so good inside. They all seemed so proud of her. She didn't remember anyone being this proud when she won races at the track in Florida. Linda was hugging her around the neck and Mikie was petting her. This was a special feeling for Twiggy. She was starting to feel like part of the family. Even Mikie seemed to be coming around and accepting her, but only more time would tell for sure.

Chapter 7 — *THE POND*

During the next couple of days, Twiggy couldn't wait for Linda and Mikie to come home from school. She looked forward to the weekend so she could spend all day with them. When Saturday finally came, a cloudy sky greeted Twiggy when she looked out the window. There were white flakes falling to the ground. It was a strange sight for her.

"What are you looking at, Twiggy?" Linda asked. "Oh, you see the snow falling. You probably never saw snow in Florida," Linda said as she patted Twiggy's head. So this is what her trainer meant when he said it snowed in Pennsylvania.

"Let's get you ready to go outside. You are coming with us to the pond. We're going ice skating. I have an old sweatshirt you can wear. I cut the sleeves short for you," Linda said.

Mikie walked into Linda's room as she was pinning the sweatshirt to fit the back of Twiggy's thin waist.

"She looks ridiculous," Mikie said as he flopped on Linda's bed.

"I think she looks adorable," replied Linda. "And everyone else will think so too," she added.

"Well, let's get going," Mikie said as he was walking out of the room. "Everyone is waiting at the pond for us."

As Twiggy walked outside, she sniffed the snow and licked it. It was so cold on her tongue and so soft and cool under her paws. She wasn't sure how to walk in it.

"Come on you silly thing. Wait until you see the ice on the pond," Linda laughed.

As Twiggy, Linda, and Mikie walked through the woods to the pond, Twiggy thought to herself how beautiful everything looked. This was certainly a new sight for her. The ground was like a pure white blanket and the trees looked as if they were covered with powdered sugar. Just the other day, Linda had shared a cookie with her that was covered with powdered sugar. But the snow didn't taste as sweet as the sugar on the cookie.

As they came near to the pond, Kenny yelled out to them, "Twiggy looks cool with that sweatshirt on. I think I'll put one of my old ones on Max."

"See! I told you," Linda said to Mikie. "Why do you always have to be so critical of Twiggy?" Linda asked as

Mikie walked away from her and Twiggy.

The boys were sweeping the snow off of the ice so they could start the game. Linda took Twiggy over to where Becky was.

"Hi Becky. I'm so glad you could come," Linda said.

"Twiggy looks so cute in your old sweatshirt. I think it looks better on her than it did on you," Becky said.

"I think you're right," Linda giggled.

Twiggy looked at the ice on the pond. She walked over to the edge of the pond and stepped gently onto the slippery surface. It looked like glass to Twiggy. It felt as hard as glass, but it was so much colder. Linda waited until Twiggy got halfway onto the pond and then she called her back. Linda knew Twiggy would come when she called and she wanted to see her slide on the ice. As Twiggy turned around and started to run back to Linda, she knew this was a different feeling under her long, skinny legs. As she got close to the edge of the pond, she tried to stop. Her claws dug into the ice. You could hear the scraping of her nails as she tried to stop herself from slipping and sliding. Linda and Becky laughed.

"You'll get used to it, Twiggy," Linda assured her. Linda and Becky were sitting around the fire the boys had built for them. They were watching the hockey game. Twiggy and Max were laying close to the fire, sleeping soundly. They were worn out from chasing the boys back and forth on the ice.

"Mikie, don't get too close to that end of the pond. The ice is thin over there and the water is deep," Linda yelled out.

"I know, I can hear it cracking. I'm coming back," Mikie yelled.

Just as Mikie turned to skate back the other way, there was a loud crack and the ice separated under his feet so fast he didn't have a chance to skate away. Into the freezing water he slid! As Mikie was sinking down, Linda and Becky were screaming, "Somebody grab him before he goes under!"

Kenny yelled back, "We can't get to him. The ice is too thin and we're too heavy. We'll all go under!"

Twiggy and Max were awakened by the screaming. Twiggy saw Mikie in the water and knew he was in trouble. She ran across the ice to where Mikie was. The ice started to make little cracking noises, but Twiggy wasn't frightened. She knew he needed help and she was the only one who was

light enough to get close to Mikie. She slowly edged her way across the slippery ice. She kept going until she could get close enough to grab the back of Mikie's jacket. She got a good grip on the back of his collar, and pulled and pulled as hard as she could. She kept pulling until he started to slowly come up out of the water. Finally, she pulled him onto the thicker ice. Everyone was cheering for Twiggy and saying how brave she was. Mikie was shaking and shivering all over, partly from being so scared and partly from being so cold. Kenny and the other boys carried Mikie over to the fire. Twiggy was following closely. She wanted to be sure he was all right.

"You have a great dog here, Mikie," Kenny and the other boys agreed.

"I know. She's the best dog in the world!" Mikie replied as he hugged Twiggy's neck.

Twiggy knew she had finally won Mikie's heart completely.

All through the rest of the winter, Mikie, Linda and Twiggy had the best of times. Twiggy went everywhere with them. Mikie really understood for the first time what the statement, "You can't judge a book by its cover," meant, and knew he finally felt it in his heart. It doesn't matter what you look like on the outside, it's what you are on the inside that counts.

Thanks to a special program, Twiggy and other dogs like her, have happy homes. She surely is a winner now.

*If you would like information
on how to adopt a greyhound,
call National Greyhound Adoption
at 1-800-348-2517.*